Where's Tweetums?

Kim and her brother were both struggling to pull Squeeze Me off Mrs. Updegraff's leg.

Suddenly, the giant snake uncoiled and went slithering off through the shrubbery.

Mrs. Updegraff, however, went right on shrieking.

"Tweetums! Where's Tweetums?" she screamed. "What's happened to my little dog?"

All eyes turned toward the Updegraffs' house. A snaky form was rearing up in the kitchen.

Oh no! gulped Oliver, his eyes widening. A bulge was working its way slowly down through the boa's body.

A shudder ran through the crowd. "Oh, my goodness!" a woman quavered in a shocked voice. *"Th-that poor little dog!"*

OLIVER'S BACK-YARD CIRCUS

MICHAEL McBRIER

Illustrated by Blanche Sims

Troll Associates

Library of Congress Cataloging in Publication Data

McBrier, Michael.
    Oliver's back-yard circus.

    Summary: A visit to the circus with his classmates
gives Oliver an idea about how to raise money for
a much needed animal shelter.
    [1. Circus—Fiction.   2. Animals—Fiction.
3. Schools—Fiction]   I. Sims, Blanche, ill.
II. Title.   III. Title: Oliver's back-yard circus.
PZ7.M122601   1987   [FIC]   86-40378
ISBN 0-8167-0822-3 (lib. bdg.)
ISBN 0-8167-0823-1 (pbk.)

OLIVER'S
BACK-YARD
CIRCUS

CHAPTER
1

Oliver Moffitt finished his orange juice in one long swallow and glanced at the kitchen clock.

"Oliver, don't gulp," said his mother. "You sound like feeding time at the zoo."

"Mmmrrrrowww! Woofwoofwoof! Arrrooooooooooow!" Oliver and Mrs. Moffitt whirled to stare at the television on the kitchen counter. It showed a yard full of dogs and cats. Pompom, Mrs. Moffitt's frisky little Shih Tzu, dashed into the room to join in the barking.

Then Kathy Kellogg, the local newsperson, appeared on the screen. "What will happen to these poor little strays?" she asked. "Right now, they're living with Mrs. Rosebury. But where will they go next?"

The camera moved to an elderly woman. "Oh, I'm sure they'll find a home somewhere," Mrs. Rosebury said hopefully.

Oliver sighed over his spoonful of oatmeal as he looked at the poor animals on the screen.

Oliver knew a lot about animals. He had his own pet-care business. Whenever anyone in the neighborhood had an animal or pet that needed boarding, they came to Oliver Moffitt. Oliver had kept many a strange creature in his home. But after pet-sitting a baby alligator who chewed up the living room, his mother made a new rule. Their house—even the garage—was off-limits to all forms of animal life except for Pom-pom.

The dogs in Mrs. Rosebury's yard jumped up and down happily. Two of the cats rubbed against her legs.

"Your neighbors call what's happening here a public nuisance." Kathy Kellogg had to shout to make herself heard over the yapping. "Now the court has given you ten days to do something about it."

"Something is going to be done," Mrs. Rosebury said. She beckoned to someone off camera. "This nice young lady has offered to help."

"Mom!" Oliver gasped. "That's Sam!" Samantha Lawrence was Oliver's next-door neighbor and best friend. She gave a nervous smile and opened her mouth to speak.

But Oliver didn't get to hear what Sam said.

As he stared in astonishment, the spoon fell from his hand, dumping hot oatmeal onto Pom-pom's back. Howling, the little dog dashed away.

Oliver jumped from the table, knocking over his bowl, and dove after Pom-pom. "Hold still,

I'll clean you—*ack!*" Oliver and half the room got spattered with oatmeal as Pom-pom suddenly stopped and shook.

By the time he and his mother had cleaned things up, Kathy Kellogg was asking Sam, "But how are you going to help Mrs. Rosebury?"

"We—some of the kids in my class and I—have a plan." Sam sounded embarrassed, which was weird. Sam *never* got embarrassed. She was the best athlete in Oliver's class, ready to turn cartwheels and do back flips at the drop of a hat. But not now.

"Yes?" said Kathy Kellogg.

"Well, it's kind of a secret," Sam said.

Mrs. Moffitt stared across the table. "Oliver," she said.

"Yes, Mom?"

"I didn't like the sound of that. What did Sam mean, 'It's a secret'? What are you two cooking up?"

Oliver shook his head. "I don't know, Mom. We're not cooking anything up. Honest."

That was true. Oliver was just as uneasy as his mother was about Sam's secret plan. How did she expect to help Mrs. Rosebury find a home for all those stray dogs and cats? He hoped Sam really had a good plan up her sleeve. The idea of the dogcatcher—or "animal-control officer," as he was known around town—coming to take them away was too sickening to think about.

"Well, we'll be following the progress of this

mysterious plan," said Kathy Kellogg. "Until then, it's back to the news room."

Oliver gulped down what was left of his oatmeal. Then he helped clear the breakfast table while his mother finished dressing for the office. She worked as a bookkeeper for an insurance company. His father lived in another city. Oliver hadn't seen him in a long time.

Mrs. Moffitt came into the kitchen and shook her head. "We'd better hurry up, Oliver. You don't want to be late—isn't this the day you're going to the circus?"

The bus was standing in front of the school, echoing with shouts and laughter as the students piled aboard.

"Think there'll be any animal acts?" Matthew Farley asked Oliver as they climbed in.

"Well, of course there'll be animal acts," said Oliver. "That's what circuses are all about!"

"Not always," said Matthew. "What about acrobats and clowns and shooting people out of cannons?"

Oliver shrugged. He wasn't sure Sneed's Super Circus would be very fancy. It had been set up near the shopping mall, a few miles from Oliver's hometown of Bartlett Woods.

Sam had already seen the show, and said it was just a small-time traveling carnival. As he saw her sitting alone, staring glumly out the window, Oliver guessed she wasn't too eager to see Sneed's Super Circus again.

He sat down in the seat beside her. "Hey, Sam. I saw you on TV this morning."

"So did Ms. Callahan," said Sam. "She asked about my plan."

"What did you tell her?"

"Nothing! I didn't have anything to *tell*!" Sam said. "It's all so stupid. I know Mrs. Rosebury because she's a friend of the Cat Lady."

Oliver nodded. He knew the Cat Lady too. She went around Bartlett Woods with a red wagon, feeding and helping the stray cats in town.

"Well, she had to go away for a while, and she left her cats with Mrs. Rosebury. That's when the neighbors started to complain," Sam said. "I went over to ask if she needed help, and the next thing I knew I was on TV."

Sam groaned and slapped her forehead. "How could I have been so dumb! Telling Kathy Kellogg our class had a secret plan to help—I just made it all up!"

"No problem," said Oliver. "We'll come up with something. And the kids will be glad to help out."

"But how can they?"

"Well . . . I don't know. They could do odd jobs or something like that. And then give Mrs. Rosebury part of what they earn."

Sam shook her head. "What good'll that do? Suppose we could talk everyone into getting a job, which I'll bet we can't. Whatever money we raised would just go for food to keep those poor cats and dogs alive for a while longer. The real problem is Mrs. Rosebury's neighbors—they don't want her keeping animals in her back yard."

Sam sighed, and they both sank into a gloomy silence.

But as the bus drew near the circus grounds, Oliver began to feel a surge of excitement. Lots of people were milling around, even this early in the day. Brightly colored flags and silver balloons fluttered overhead, while rock music blared from loudspeakers.

The bus stopped and the driver opened the doors.

Oliver's heart beat faster as he and his classmates filed out of the bus and started through the ticket gate.

"Where are you going first?" asked Matthew once they were inside the circus grounds.

Oliver paused to take in the scene. A good-sized tent served as the show's Big Top. Rides and games and refreshment stands lay before them. At the far end of the grounds was a cluster of wagons and wheeled cages.

"Guess!" he said, heading straight for the cages.

There weren't a lot of animals, but Oliver stared with fascination into every cage and pen. Two white horses and a zebra were fenced off to one side, chewing happily on some wisps of hay. Sophie the elephant was on the other side, spraying herself with water from her trunk. A game of tag was going on in the monkey cage, and a chimp was making faces at all the people who'd lined up to look at him.

Oliver walked to the next cage, where the lion stalked back and forth. He flicked his tail and glared out at the people with his yellow eyes. Next door was a bored tiger lying on his side with his eyes almost closed.

Oliver stared at the tiger. The tiger opened its eyes, twitched its tail, and bared its fangs.

"What a magnificent creature!" Oliver exclaimed.

The tiger yawned and tossed its head.

Oliver took a deep breath. His eyes glazed over dreamily. First he thought of what he would do if he were chief animal tender of Sneed's Super Circus. Then grander visions began to pass through his mind. . . .

Oliver imagined himself in safari garb with a tropical sun helmet on his head. He was overseeing a vast game preserve in Africa or India. It was his mission to show the world how an experienced pet-care expert could re-stock all the wildlife areas!

Oliver went on daydreaming. He was just climbing into a jeep with a couple of Waziri trackers to go after a gang of elephant-tusk thieves, when a voice said, "Oliver, are you all right?"

"Huh?" Oliver turned to see Sam standing beside him.

"You had the funniest look on your face," she said.

"I was thinking."

"Did you come up with a plan to help Mrs. Rosebury?" Sam asked hopefully.

"Uh, no," said Oliver. "I'm still working on that."

Sam looked very serious. "When I think of all those poor dogs and cats—you know what happens if they're caught."

Oliver nodded. "What this town needs is—"

He broke off as the tiger suddenly flicked one ear and let out a bellow. The animal sprang to its feet in one powerful surge. A fearsome roar rumbled up from deep in its throat.

"What happened?" gasped Sam.

"Something hit that tiger on the ear," said Oliver, whirling around. "And I think I know what!"

"What?"

"A bean."

"A *bean*? Why do you think that?"

"Because one just hit *me* on the nose!"

"Don't be silly. . . ." But Sam stopped when she turned around and saw what Oliver was talking about.

Rusty Jackson stood a few yards away, near the elephant pen, with a big pink teddy bear under one arm. He held a gold bean shooter in one hand and a bag of plastic beans in the other.

"That jerk!" said Sam.

Rusty was the school bully. Oliver could guess where he got that teddy bear. He'd probably blown all his money at the games.

Sam flared at him, "That's just your speed,

Rusty Jackson—shooting beans at sweet little animals!"

"Yeah, well, you talk big here," said Rusty. "But you looked pretty stupid on TV this morning. A secret plan to help the animals—give me a break!"

With a hoot of laughter he aimed another bean in their direction. Then he shot several at the zebra and one at Sophie the elephant.

"What a creep!" Sam muttered.

Rusty turned around, loaded his bean shooter, and pointed it at her. But just as he was about to shoot, a gallon of water splashed him in the face.

Rusty jumped as the whole crowd started laughing.

"How about that?" said Oliver. "Sophie's getting even!"

The elephant sucked up another trunkful of water from her drinking trough. And before Rusty could duck, she sprayed him again.

"Stupid animals!" Rusty yelled as he ran off, dripping wet.

Laughing, Sam and Oliver headed toward the midway. They wandered from stand to stand. Sam took a chance at pitching baseballs, and Oliver bought them each a giant cone of cotton candy. They watched people shoot at wooden ducks. Then they went on the Crack-the-Whip ride, and the bumper cars. Afterward, they ate hot dogs for lunch.

Outside the Big Top they saw the performers

begin to harness the horses and deck Sophie out in fancy trappings.

"Come on!" Oliver exclaimed. "Looks like the show's about to start."

They went inside and found seats next to Matthew Farley and Josh Burns, the smartest boy in their class. They all held their breath as the spotlights blazed down on the center ring. Then the performers came trooping in, led by a five-piece band.

There were the usual capering clowns and pretty showgirls. One young woman rode Sophie the elephant while others perched on the white horses as they galloped around the ring. A high-wire act followed. Then the lion tamer put two big cats through their paces.

Oliver sat through it all, spellbound by the wonder of the show. *How did they do it?* he marveled. An idea began to bubble around in his brain.

All it takes is a tent, some music, a few flashy costumes, and some eye-catching acts. Come right down to it, the music could just as well be canned. And the acts don't have to be all that good, either.

Maybe even a tent isn't absolutely necessary...

Oliver was still under the spell of the Big Top on the bus going home. He had grabbed a seat next to Sam, but hardly a word passed between them. Oliver stared in glazed-eyed silence, wrapped in deep thought.

"Hey," Sam said, "snap out of it, Oliver!"

"Huh? . . . Snap out of what?"

"Your trance."

Sam was waving her hand up and down in front of his face.

"I just had the best idea of my life," Oliver said, grinning. "Sam, are you ready for this? I think I've just solved our problem about how to help Mrs. Rosebury and her strays!"

Sam looked hopeful but unconvinced. "Okay, tell me."

Oliver rubbed his hands together. "What Bartlett Woods needs is an animal shelter. And we're going to raise the money to build one."

"We're going to do this?" Sam said. "How?"

"Simple. We put on a circus!"

CHAPTER 2

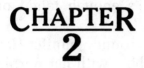

"**O**liver, are you nuts?" Sam said. "How are we going to put on a circus?"

"Easy. We get some animals and work up some acts. Josh will use his computer to make signs. All we have to do is sell tickets and—well, like that." Oliver spread his hands and smiled.

Sam still didn't look quite sure.

"I'll bet we'll make lots of money—enough to build a real animal shelter, so all the strays in town have a place to stay."

Sam shook her head. "Oliver, where do you get these ideas?"

Oliver shrugged modestly. "It takes practice, I guess. But once you get in the habit of thinking up great ideas, more keep coming."

"Hmm," said Sam. "What do we do about getting acts? Or do you have an idea about that too?"

Oliver smiled. "No problem. After they hear about our talent search, we'll have people begging to be in our show." He spread his arms. "I'll bet there's enough talent on this bus to make a circus!"

Sam stared around. Jennifer Hayes was blowing a huge bubble with her purple bubble gum. It was almost as big as her head. Kim Williams was trying to balance her circus pennant on its pole, but the pole fell over, bursting Jennifer's bubble.

Sam shook her head. "A talent search?" She sounded doubtful.

They were still talking about the circus as they walked home. "There's something that still worries me," said Sam. "Where are we going to stage the show?"

"That's a good question," said Oliver. "We'll have to look into it."

On Saturday, Sam waylaid Oliver as he was bringing Pom-pom home from his morning walk. "Well, have you looked into it?"

"Looked into what?"

"Where we're going to hold the show," Sam said. "If you haven't, we should start now."

Oliver put Pom-pom inside the house, and was just starting off with Sam when he heard someone calling him.

"Hey, Oliver!" A little five-year-old boy came running from the house next door.

Oliver sighed. "Oh, hi, Andrew," he said. Andrew Finch was Oliver's next-door neighbor.

"Where are you going?" Andrew asked.

"Away," said Oliver. The last thing he wanted was Andrew tagging along with him. Out of the corner of his mouth he muttered to Sam, "Come on! Let's go before he gets any ideas!"

"Can I come?" said Andrew.

"No," answered Oliver without looking around. He and Sam raced to the end of the block.

"Uh-oh," said Sam as they turned the corner.

"What's the matter?"

"We've got company."

Andrew was running after them.

"I thought I told you you couldn't come along," Oliver said when he caught up.

"It's okay," said Andrew. "I told Mom I was going for a walk with you and Sam, and she said it was all right."

Oliver and Sam looked at each other helplessly. Oliver sighed. "Okay, if you can keep up. Just try not to be too much of a pest, please."

"What's a pest?" said Andrew.

"Wait a while, and I'll show you," said Oliver.

They walked toward Arrowhead Park, which was mostly woods—not a good place for a circus. But just beyond the edge of the park was a vacant lot. It had a wooden building on it that looked like an old garage. Otherwise the lot was bare.

"The town used to park their clean-up trucks here, but they don't use it anymore," Oliver said. "We'd have plenty of room for the circus. And afterward, if we made enough money, we could put up a wire fence, and this could be the animal shelter too."

Sam looked around. "Lots of trash here," she said.

"And broken glass—Andrew, get away from that!" Oliver grabbed Andrew's hand and pulled him away from a smashed soda bottle.

"I wanna go exploring," Andrew protested.

"How much work do you think it would take to clean this up?" Oliver asked.

"Too much—if we're trying to get the circus ready too," Sam said.

Andrew tugged at the leg of Oliver's jeans.

"Can't talk now," said Oliver. "Sam and I are busy."

Andrew tugged again.

Oliver frowned at him. "Remember you asked me what a pest is?"

"Is that one over there?" Andrew said.

"What?"

"A pest—over there."

Andrew pointed. Oliver looked. Then he looked again. An animal was peering out at them from the trees and bushes at the edge of the park.

"Good grief," said Sam. "What is it?"

"It's a dog—I think." Oliver stared. The animal *looked* like a dog—sort of. But Oliver had to admit that he'd never seen a blue dog before.

He stepped a little closer. Yes. The dog *was* blue, slate blue, and he didn't seem to have much hair. He was also big. He was almost as big as Wally Perona's dog, Bruiser.

But that wasn't all. The dog's head was too big for his body. His bloodshot little eyes and jagged bulldoggy fangs would certainly scare the wits out of any burglar. Yet his sad, wrinkled, droopy face made him seem gentle and kind of funny.

"Don't let my looks fool you, folks," he seemed to be begging. "I'm really not as weird as I look. Please be friends with me."

"It looks like something from another planet," Sam said.

"I think he's some kind of mastiff," said Oliver. "I saw a picture like that in my dog book. Hey—!"

He lunged forward just in time to grab Andrew by the T-shirt. He was darting toward the strange dog.

"I wanna pet the doggie!" Andrew screeched. He tried to wriggle out of Oliver's clutches.

"That's not a good idea, if you haven't been introduced," said Oliver. "Some doggies bite."

The blue dog seemed to know they were talking about him. He shrank back shyly into the underbrush.

Andrew started to cry. "You scared him away!"

The blue head suddenly darted out again. It let out a loud, "*Woof!*"

Andrew tore loose and ran to the bushes. Oliver and Sam chased after him. They plunged through the bushes to a small clear space. There

stood Andrew, facing the dog. "Nice doggie," he said.

The dog put his head down.

"Oliver, that dog is on a leash," Sam said.

"Yeah," said Andrew. "Somebody tied him to that tree."

"And left him," Oliver said. "He's been here for hours—maybe days!"

"That's mean!" Andrew said. "How could he eat or get a drink of water? Let him loose, Oliver!"

The dog looked even sadder than before. But when Oliver stepped forward, the dog's head came up. He gave a warning growl.

Oliver stopped. "How can I get him loose if he won't let me near him?"

"Don't be afraid," Andrew told the dog. "We're friends. We want to help!"

"Don't let him get too close," Oliver whispered to Sam. She took firm hold of Andrew's arm.

The blue dog put his head down again. He looked at Andrew and whined. Then his stumpy tail began to wag.

Oliver reached over and untied the leash from the tree.

Quickly, the blue dog bounded away. He crashed through the bushes and disappeared.

Andrew turned to Oliver. "You let him get away!" And then he *really* started to cry.

Oliver sighed. "Come on, Andrew," he said. "I think it's time to go home."

*   *   *

Later that day Oliver and Sam were out riding their bicycles. They were still looking for a place to hold the circus. "Okay, the park and the school yard are out," said Sam. "It'll take too much time to get permission to use them. And we have only ten days to help Mrs. Rosebury."

"Well," said Oliver, "if we can't have the circus on public land, we'll have to have it on private property. Let's ask around and see if there's a back yard we can use."

They biked past Jennifer's house. She was dressed in a purple T-shirt and shorts, sitting on her front steps with Kim. When they saw Oliver and Sam, they waved and ran over.

"We've got something to ask . . ." Oliver began.

But Jennifer was already talking. "Don't you really hate it when you get new grass seed? Now we can't play in the yard. Kim's yard was seeded too." She looked up at Oliver. "So what were you going to ask?"

"Never mind," Sam sighed. "You've already answered our question."

"But you guys *will* be helping with the circus, won't you?" Oliver asked. "We need all kinds of acts. Clowns, animal trainers, trapeze artists, dancing girls."

"Okay, you've got a dancing girl right here!" Kim giggled. She snapped her fingers and started to hum and sway all the way up the walk to Jennifer's house.

"No, he's got two!" said Jennifer. She plopped down on the steps with Kim and started doing a sitting-down dance number.

"Great!" said Oliver as he and Sam went back to their bicycles. "At least it's something," he whispered as they pedaled off.

Matthew shook his head when they asked him. "I'm not allowed to have more than four friends out in the yard," he said. "So I don't think my folks would like the idea of a whole audience coming in."

Oliver and Sam looked at each other. "Will you be in the show?" Sam asked.

"Doing what?" said Matthew.

"You've been taking juggling lessons," Oliver pointed out.

"I take lessons in lots of things." Matthew looked a little embarrassed. "That doesn't mean I'm good enough."

"You'll be good enough for our circus."

Matthew thought for a moment. "When are you going to sign up the circus acts?" he asked.

"Starting tomorrow," said Oliver. "Come around to my place. If I'm not home, leave a note in the mailbox."

"Okay."

Josh's back yard was filled with all sorts of weird contraptions and inventions, so Oliver and Sam knew better than to ask him.

"We have to find someplace," Sam said as they pedaled along. Suddenly she turned to Oliver. "Psst!" she hissed, pointing. "Look over there!"

From around the corner padded the blue dog,

29

the long leash still dragging behind him. Oliver had promised Andrew that he'd keep an eye out for the dog.

"Come on! Let's try to catch him!" They turned toward the dog, but when he saw them, he turned and ran.

Oliver and Sam tried to pedal faster, but as they turned the corner, someone zoomed out from a side street and cut them off. It was Rusty, smiling his sinister smile.

"I heard about your dumb circus idea on TV," he said. "If that was your secret plan, you two must be lamer than I thought."

He leaned over his handlebars and laughed. "So where is this disaster gonna happen?"

"Well . . ." said Sam, but Oliver spoke up.

"We're going to hold it in my back yard," he said, looking Rusty in the eye.

Rusty laughed louder. "That's a real hoot. A circus—in your dinky yard." Still laughing, he pedaled off.

Sam stared. "Oliver, are you sure that's okay?"

"No problem," said Oliver. "After I explain things to Mom, she'll be glad to help."

They headed for home. But the closer Oliver came to his mother, the more he wondered what she would say.

Lunch was waiting when Oliver got home. He ate glumly while his mother listened to the news.

"And now, some more about that talent search in Bartlett Woods," said Kathy Kellogg. "If you tuned in to last night's news show, you may remember our story about the school kids who are putting on a circus. They're trying to raise money to build an animal shelter."

Oliver crammed the rest of his butterscotch pudding into his mouth and got up quickly. His mother was looking at him.

"Naturally, they need acts for their circus," Kathy Kellogg went on with a chuckle. "So if you want to break into show biz, here's your chance. The people to call are Oliver Moffitt and Samantha Lawrence."

"Oliver," said Mrs. Moffitt, "what's all this about a circus?"

"Er, just doing a little community service, Mom."

"You're not getting into something that's going to mean animals all over the house, I hope?" Oliver could see the warning in her eyes.

"Of course not," Oliver said. "There are a lot of other acts too—jugglers, clowns, dancers, all sorts of stuff."

"That's not what I asked, Oliver."

"There won't be anybody in the house," Oliver promised. "This is a back-yard circus. We'll be doing everything in the back yard. . . ."

That was as far as Oliver got.

"Oliver," Mrs. Moffitt began, "I let you pet-sit a dog, a cat, and a duck in our house. You've had gerbils, fish, and a monkey in the garage. I didn't even say much when you kept that alligator in my bathtub. But a circus in our back yard is out of the question! I can't think of one

31

good reason why I should let an audience trample everything around our house. Can you?"

"Well," said Oliver, "at least they're people, not animals . . ."

"That's not good enough!" Mrs. Moffitt said.

Oliver could see that his mother was really angry. "It's just that we need to run this circus really quickly," he said.

"So quickly that you didn't have time to ask my permission, I suppose!" said Mrs. Moffitt. "I'm sorry, Oliver, but you'll have to find another place to run this show of yours."

"But Mom . . ." Oliver started to say.

"Oliver."

Silently, Oliver put his dishes into the sink. "I think I'll go out for a while," he said, heading for the door.

Sam was chinning herself on a tree in her yard. She dropped down and ran to the fence when she saw Oliver.

"Hey, how did that stuff about our circus get on the news?" he asked her.

"I called the station," Sam said with a grin. "Got us some great free publicity—and help in finding circus acts too. Smart idea, huh?"

"Yeah—right. It was kind of a surprise, that's all."

"Did you ask your mom if we could hold the circus in your back yard?"

Oliver squirmed. "Um—not exactly."

"Oliver, we're running out of time," Sam reminded him. "The court gave Mrs. Rosebury only ten days to get rid of her pets. My mom said there was no *way* we could hold the circus over here. Do you think you can convince your mom to do it?''

"Well . . ." Oliver dug into the ground with the toe of his shoe. "No," he finally said. "I already tried, and she hates the idea. Sam, what are we going to do?''

Just then, the back door of the Moffitts' house opened. "Oliver," called his mother, "you're wanted on the telephone."

Oliver ran into the house and picked up the phone. "Hello?" he said.

"How do you do, Mr. Moffitt," said a deep voice at the other end of the line. "This is Mrs. Updegraff. I understand you're the young man who's putting on some sort of circus."

Oliver stood staring at the telephone. Everybody in Bartlett Woods knew the Updegraffs. They were the richest family in town, with a big mansion in the middle of beautiful rolling lawns.

"Hello?" said Mrs. Updegraff. "Are you there?"

"Um—yes," said Oliver. "W-what can I do for you?''

"There is something we should discuss—it's about your circus," said Mrs. Updegraff. "Could you come to my house—shall we say at two o'clock?''

"Yes, ma'am," said Oliver. "I'd like to bring Samantha Lawrence with me—we're working together on the circus."

"Very good. I shall expect you then."

Click. Mrs. Updegraff had ended her call.

Oliver hung up and wiped his hands on his jeans.

"What was that all about?" his mother asked.

"That," sighed Oliver, "is what *I'd* like to know."

CHAPTER
3

At two o'clock on the dot Oliver and Sam walked up the driveway to the Updegraff mansion. A butler answered the door and led them to the sitting room where Mrs. Updegraff was waiting.

Mrs. Updegraff was a large, stout woman who always tilted her head back so she could look down her nose at people.

"How nice of you children to come." She beamed, displaying large, shiny teeth. On her lap was a tiny Yorkshire terrier. Seated next to her was a tall, gangly teen-ager with light hair. Mrs. Updegraff stroked her dog and said, "Be nice, Tweetums." She gestured to the boy. "This is my nephew, Chad."

Chad gave the two visitors a bored, scornful look and grunted something between a "humph" and a "hi."

"I heard about your talent search on the news," Mrs. Updegraff said with a little laugh. "This immediately gave me a splendid idea!"

She patted her nephew on the shoulder. "Chad here, you see, attends the Oaktree School of Dramatic Arts. He's studying all forms of artistic expression—ballet, acting, singing, stagecraft— oh my, I don't know what all! I realized at once that his talents would add the perfect touch to your circus!"

Turning proudly to Chad, she said, "Tell them what you can do, dear."

Chad lurched up from the couch and started walking around the room. "My Persian Dervish number will fit right in. It's what you might call muscle dancing, you know—twirling dumbbells while leaping gracefully through the air. I have the most marvelous costume for it—absolutely gorgeous!"

As he talked he flapped his arms. One elbow clipped a marble pedestal and the pedestal went flying. The vase that stood on top of it went flying too. Both crashed to the floor.

"Chad!" cried Mrs. Updegraff. "That was a Ming vase! Your uncle paid thousands of dollars for it!" She sighed. "Oh, well. We have another in the library."

The butler appeared a few seconds later with a dustpan and brush. "Third thing he's destroyed today," Oliver heard him mutter as he swept up the pieces.

Chad went on talking as if nothing had happened. "*I'll* be the circus strong man and lead the parade into the ring. Then I'll top it all off by belting out a song."

"And, of course, *I'll* see that Kathy Kellogg and her camera crew are there, catching it all on tape," Mrs. Updegraff added. "Chad will be able to use it later as a demo tape for Broadway."

"Gee, that's a terrific idea!" said Oliver. He shook his head sadly. "There's just one problem."

Chad scowled. "What's that?"

"We can't find anyplace to hold the show." Oliver turned to Sam. She was staring at the huge rolling lawns outside the window. That's when the idea hit him. "So there may not be a circus at all," he continued. "Unless . . ."

"Unless what?"

"Unless you would allow us to stage it right here in your yard . . . but—that's out," Oliver corrected himself hastily. "Who'd want a crowd of people trampling over their grass!"

With a sigh, Oliver ended, "Too bad. I'll bet your dance routine at the head of the parade would've been sensational, Chad."

"Aunt Augusta . . ." Chad looked anxiously at Mrs. Updegraff.

Sam and Oliver could see her struggling bravely with the idea of letting a crowd into her yard.

"Oh, I don't know," she said slowly, trying hard to smile. "I—I don't see what's so terrible about the idea. In fact, yes—you may hold your circus right here in my yard."

*   *   *

Oliver and Sam bicycled away happily from the Updegraff mansion. "Boy, you're something else, Oliver!" Sam said, grinning. "How do you do it?"

"Easy." Oliver grinned back. "When opportunity knocks, I open the door." But Oliver stopped grinning when he reached his house. A crowd of kids was lined up in the driveway.

His mother stood outside with a wild look in her eyes. "They started arriving right after you left. I thought I told you—"

"Hey!" interrupted a boy. "Are you the guy running the circus? Listen to this!"

He pulled out a trumpet and put it to his lips. *Blaaaaatttttt!* Oliver was almost deafened. Mrs. Moffitt looked as if she were about to wrap the trumpet around the boy's neck.

"I'm sorry, Mom," Oliver said quickly. "We'll only have the auditions here today—and I'll keep everybody in the driveway."

Mrs. Moffitt went back inside, sighing. "I don't know how I get into these things. . . ."

Oliver and Sam went to the front of the line. "Have I got an act for you," said a boy, holding up a black box with the word DANGER printed on it.

"What's that?" Sam said a little nervously.

"The greatest circus act of all time, that's all." The boy began opening the box. "Stand back now. He's a killer."

Oliver peeked into the box. "That's just a frog!"

"Yeah, but wait till you see what he does to flies," said the boy.

"Yes—well, I don't think this is a very good act for the younger members of our audience." Oliver sent the boy and his killer frog home.

Next in line was a little boy balancing an apple on his head. "Is that your act?" Oliver asked.

"No, he's just my assistant," said a girl in the line. She stood proudly with a bow and arrows.

Sam looked from the arrows to the apple on the little boy's head. "No way," she said. "This act is too dangerous."

"No, it's not," the girl said. "My mom won't let me use real arrows. These just have a little rubber cup on the tip. But it's still a great act!" She aimed an arrow at her assistant's head and fired. The arrow hit the Moffitts' garage door. Oliver and Sam looked at each other and sighed.

The screen door opened, and Pom-pom came scampering out. He cocked his head to one side, looking at the line. Then he ran over beside Oliver and bravely started barking at everyone.

Kim Williams came up with Jennifer, her eyes sparkling with excitement. "I talked to my brother Parnell, and he says it's okay," she said. "How's this for an act? I'm going to dance with Squeeze Me!"

Squeeze Me was Parnell's boa constrictor—and Kim was carrying him on her shoulders. The snake wriggled around, trying to see what was happening. His head was around Kim's knee—

and standing right in front of him was Pom-pom. For a long moment the snake looked down at the dog—and the dog looked up at the snake. Then, howling, Pom-pom made a beeline back to the door.

"He runs pretty fast when he wants to, doesn't he?" said Sam. "Hey, Oliver, why don't you teach Pom-pom some tricks for the show?"

"Pom-pom?" Oliver made a face. "You've got to be joking."

"I mean simple stuff, like sitting up and begging, or jumping through a hoop."

Oliver shook his head. "Pom-pom's hopeless. I already tried when my mother first got him. He seems to think people exist just to feed and pamper him."

Kim was jumping up and down. "So what do you think of my act?"

"How are you going to dance with Squeeze Me?" Oliver asked.

"You know that graceful bit girls do on a mat at gymnastics meets?" said Kim. "Each one performs to her own special music. Well, I've been practicing a routine like that. Only now I'll work Squeeze Me into the act."

"How?" said Sam.

"Get him to twine around me and like, you know, sway in time to the music."

"Wow! I think Squeeze Me could be the hit of the show!" said Oliver.

"But what about me?" Jennifer asked.

"Tell you what!" said Oliver. "Sam's going

to do acrobatics, and she'll need a partner. You can perform with her!"

Jennifer looked pleased. "Sounds okay to me."

But Sam was looking at Oliver. "Since when am I doing acrobatics?"

"Well, you're the best athlete in our class, aren't you?"

Sam shrugged. "I don't know. I like sports."

"So you're the perfect one to do an acrobatic act. Look," Oliver added quickly, "this won't be the Olympics. All you'd have to do is a few of those stunts you do real well."

"Like what?"

"Oh, flips and somersaults—maybe walking up steps on your hands. You know—stuff like that." Oliver scratched his head thoughtfully and went on. "Maybe we could borrow the Smythes' portable gym so you could do some fancy twirls. In fact, we might even rig a high wire for you to walk on with a balancing pole."

"High wire!" Sam looked horrified. "Are you kidding?"

"Well, not all that high." Oliver held up one hand to his face. "Maybe about here—just high enough to look scary."

"You think it wouldn't be? I could still land hard if I fell!"

"Well, you'll have a partner to help you."

"Oooooh," said Jennifer. "Sounds exciting."

Sam shook her head. "Yeah. Real exciting."

"So," Oliver went on, "we have two great acts. But we need some more animals." He raised his voice. "Does anyone here have an animal act?"

"Right here." Josh Burns took out a drawing on a piece of paper. "The show's now got a giraffe."

Oliver looked at the drawing. "What's this?"

"Our giraffe costume. Mine and Tim's."

"Tim B.?"

"Yeah."

"Tim's pretty shy," said Sam. "He hardly ever raises his hand in class, even when he knows the answer. How do you expect to get him to perform in our circus?"

"I already asked him. He said he would. I told him we'd be inside the costume, and nobody would see us."

"Now that you mention it, how will you guys see?"

"Tim won't have to," said Josh. "I'll be the front end."

"But the neck goes up so high. How can you see?"

"Through a periscope. It'll stick up through the giraffe's neck the way a submarine periscope does underwater."

"Great," said Oliver. "Any more animals?"

"Right here." Wally Perona stepped forward.

Wally was the biggest boy in school. And his dog, Bruiser, had to be the biggest dog in Bartlett Woods. He was part St. Bernard, part sheep dog, and part Great Dane. Bruiser had been Oliver's first customer when he started his pet-care business.

"What kind of act is it?" Sam asked.

"You'll see," Wally said proudly. He pulled what looked like a bundle of black string from a bag. "Wait till I get his mane on."

"Don't tell me," Oliver said. "Bruiser is going to be a lion?"

"Right," said Wally. "This used to be a mop until I dyed it with black ink. Now all I have to do is tie it around under his chin." He looked at Oliver. "Hold him still for a minute."

"Are you out of your mind? I can't hold this monster."

"Well, try."

Oliver squatted in front of Bruiser and tried to hold him while Wally tied the mop. "See?" he said. "Is he fierce, or what?"

Bruiser leaped forward, knocking Oliver down. He put his paws on Oliver's shoulders and started licking his face.

"Really fierce." Sam laughed as she tried to tug Bruiser away so Oliver could get up.

As he got back to his feet, Oliver said, "Too bad the Fence Lady sent Houdini away."

The Fence Lady was a former client named Arabella—and Houdini was the pet camel she kept out of sight behind a high fence. Oliver had secretly taken care of Houdini while Arabella was away. But now Houdini was back in North Africa with his mother.

"We could have charged for a ride around the yard," Oliver went on.

"Plus souvenir snapshots," Sam added.

Oliver sighed. "We would have cleaned up!"

"Hi!" A gawky, fair-haired kid came walking up the drive. Oliver's heart sank as he recognized Chad Updegraff.

"Hey, clever," said Chad, pointing toward Bruiser. "A lion, huh? But his mane's crooked. It hangs down over one ear." He grabbed hold of the mop head. "Now, if you just twist it this way . . . oops!"

Bruiser howled and jumped. Chad went flying, landing flat on his back. Wally Perona loomed over him.

"Hey! What are you trying to do?" Wally said angrily. "Strangle my dog?"

He turned to Oliver. "Who *is* that creep?"

"Shhhh," said Oliver. "That's Mrs. Updegraff's nephew, Chad. She promised we could hold the circus in her yard if we put him in the show."

"Boy, did you get the short end of *that* deal!"

"Listen, I *had* to agree," Oliver argued. "Without his aunt's yard there wouldn't be any circus. If he backs out, there goes our show!"

"Don't worry," said Sam. "Something tells me he's too eager to see himself muscle dancing on video tape to ever call it off."

Oliver sighed. "Let's hope you're right."

"Don't worry, Oliver," said Wally. "This will be a great show. Wait till I train Bruiser to roar and jump through a hoop when I crack the whip. He'll bring the house down!"

"That's what I'm afraid of," said Sam.

CHAPTER
4

After two more days of auditions, Oliver was glad for any excuse to get away. He couldn't believe the weird things people thought would make great circus acts.

So, when Sam suggested that he should meet Mrs. Rosebury, he hopped right on his bike and followed her.

They found Mrs. Rosebury in her back yard, feeding her collection of strays. "Oh, how nice to see you," she said to Sam. "And you must be Oliver Moffitt."

Oliver smiled as dogs and cats crowded around him, sniffing and rubbing against his legs. He bent down to pat an old golden retriever who happily licked his hand.

"Is everyone leaving you in peace?" Sam asked.

"Oh, yes, indeed! I believe this circus you

two are putting on has changed everyone's attitude. People call and send me money to feed my pets, and I get interviewed on TV every day. A gentleman from the town council even stopped by to talk to me. You've done so much good!''

Sam reached out to squeeze Oliver's hand. Oliver crossed two fingers for luck, knowing they had a long way to go.

"Well, we hope that the circus will be a big help,'' he said.

"By the way, would you like a couple of trained animals for your circus?'' Mrs. Rosebury asked.

"*Would* we?'' said Oliver eagerly. "What have you got?''

"Well, there's Pierre for one. I'll show you.''

Mrs. Rosebury went into the house and came out with a little clown's cap and white ruff. She called to a fuzzy gray middle-sized dog, who scampered over to meet the visitors. He shook hands with Sam and Oliver. Then after Mrs. Rosebury put the ruff around his neck and the hat on his head, he sat up and begged and walked around on his hind legs.

"Pierre's wonderful!'' Sam laughed, clapping her hands. The dog wagged his tail.

"It's the poodle in him,'' said Mrs. Rosebury. "I have a little flag you can tie to his paw when he marches. He even used to dance with me when I was spry enough to bend down and hold his little hands—I mean paws.''

"I'll come and pick him up first thing Saturday morning for the show,'' said Oliver. "Okay?''

"Yes, indeed, that'll be fine. And there's also Jack Dempsey, my boxing cat. Would you like to see him?"

"We sure would!"

She led them over to a gaunt, battle-scarred old tomcat, who was dozing on the back porch. Mrs. Rosebury dangled her locket in front of him. The cat reared up on his hind legs and began punching at it with both front paws.

"Oh, how cute!" Sam laughed.

"I remember a man who used to train a whole team of cat boxers and went around putting on shows," said Mrs. Rosebury. "They actually wore little boxing gloves."

"Say, do you have any other cat who'll box with Jack?" Oliver asked.

Mrs. Rosebury sighed. "I used to. But now the other cats are all too old or fat or lazy. Besides, they know Jack's too fast with his paws, so they don't even try."

Oliver was wrapped in thought as they walked away from Mrs. Rosebury's. "Do you suppose we could talk Jennifer into matching her cat, Princess Fluffy, against Jack?"

Sam grinned. "I doubt it. No harm in asking, though, I guess."

On their way to the auditions they stopped by the Hayes's house. While the two girls chatted, Oliver tied a key on a string and dangled it in front of Jennifer's cat. Princess Fluffy was bored and languid at first, but soon began to bat the key with one paw, then the other. Soon she sat up and began batting with both paws.

"What're you doing?" Jennifer asked Oliver.

"Teaching Princess Fluffy to box. How'd you like to star her in a boxing match with another cat?"

"No way," Jennifer said firmly.

"Oh, come on," said Oliver. "It's just play-fighting. Wouldn't you like to have her in the show with you?"

"Well-l-l . . ." said Jennifer.

"We can even have little boxing gloves for the cats," Oliver said. "That way you'll know there's no danger of Princess Fluffy getting scratched."

Jennifer looked tempted, but shook her head. "I don't think so."

"Look, I'll make the boxing gloves myself," said Oliver.

"I just don't know," Jennifer said.

"They'll be purple boxing gloves," said Oliver. He knew that purple was Jennifer's favorite color, just like her favorite band was the Purple Worms. "In fact, I'll even buy a Purple Worms necklace for Fluffy to wear."

Jennifer smiled. "Okay," she said.

"What a slick operator!" Sam giggled as they left the house.

"At least I got the dumb cat," Oliver muttered.

After that first day Oliver had managed to hold the auditions in the Updegraffs' drive. He'd told Chad that he needed his "years of theatrical training" to help judge the acts.

And several more acts had been added to the program. Ambrose Magee, a fourth-grader, volunteered to be a clown on stilts. Matthew was not only working hard on his juggling act, he'd also come across a gorilla suit his father had once worn to a masquerade party. It was too big for any of their classmates, but Oliver had high hopes of talking Wally Perona into wearing it.

Linda Jaworsky in the seventh grade offered to show off her baton-twirling. When she wouldn't be twirling her baton, she'd walk around with a tray, peddling popcorn.

Carmela Payton from the sixth grade showed up with a unicycle. Somebody in her family had bought it in a junk shop. It needed a little fixing, and Chad had almost broken it when he first got his hands on it. And Carmela still wasn't good at balancing on the thing. But Oliver added her to their line-up of circus stars.

The performers had agreed to provide their own costumes. They were even going to help with refreshments. The boys promised to make popcorn, and the girls said they'd make lemonade.

Meanwhile, Josh had turned out a bunch of signs and flyers on his word processor. He and Matthew and some other kids delivered the flyers house-to-house, all through the neighborhood.

So, when Oliver and Sam pedaled up, they saw a real show taking shape. Kids were hard at work rehearsing. The only bad part was Chad walking among them, giving advice.

"Carmela," he told the girl on the unicycle, "you'd have a lot more stage presence if you leaned back a little. People would see your face."

Carmela leaned back—and promptly flipped off the unicycle. "Thanks a lot, you big jerk," she said, rubbing her shoulder.

Chad walked over to Matthew, who was practicing his juggling. "Remember what I told you? It's all in the timing," Chad said. "Now, count with me—one-two-three, one-two-three . . ."

One of Matthew's mother's plates flew high into the air and landed with a crash in the driveway. As Matthew frantically tried to get control again, a saucer and a cup crashed too.

Chad nodded encouragingly. "Much better," he said. Then he strolled over to where Ambrose Magee was wobbling on his stilts. "Would you like some advice, Ambrose?" he called up.

"Would you like a punch in the nose, Chad?" Ambrose growled down.

"Well," said Chad, "there are some people who appreciate what I have to tell them."

"Yeah," Sam whispered. "If they live through it."

Chad hurried over when he saw Oliver and Sam. "Things are looking good," he said. "But when are we going to have the dress rehearsal?"

Oliver plowed his fingers through his hair. "I don't know. I don't think we'll have the time for one."

Chad looked shocked. "You mean you'd be crazy enough to put on a show without running through it even once to see if it works?"

Oliver had a secret feeling that he and Sam might be just that crazy. It was hard enough to get the kids together for the show itself, much less a dress rehearsal. Aside from that, they both were haunted by the fear that something might go wrong that would wreck the whole Saturday circus before it started.

On Thursday afternoon Oliver came home with dragging feet. He went into the garage and began straightening up some of the circus props he'd stored in there.

"Oliver?" a voice said behind him.

Oliver turned around to find Andrew standing behind him. He had a sandwich in his hand. His mouth was smeared with peanut butter and jelly, and his cheeks looked tear-stained.

"Did you find him?" Andrew asked hopefully.

Oliver blinked for second, then remembered. "No, Andrew, I'm sorry. I haven't seen that blue dog since the day we chased him on the bicycles."

"And you let him get away. *Again*." Tears were starting to roll down Andrew's face. "You've got to find that blue doggie! He looked so sad."

"Well, a couple of other kids have seen him around the neighborhood. As soon as the show is over, we'll go looking for him. Okay?"

"O-okay." Andrew's chin quivered. "Promise?"

"I promise. Now go back home."

Andrew headed out of the garage, and Oliver turned back to tidying things up.

Then, behind him, he heard a shrill cry.

"Andrew, what's wrong?" Oliver asked, hurrying out of the garage.

Rusty Jackson was strolling up the drive with a dog on a leash. The dog had a wrinkled, fangy face and was definitely blue.

"It's Blue Doggie!" screamed Andrew.

"No, it's not. His name's Yuck," said Rusty. "How do you like him?"

"Boy, he's something else!" said Oliver.

"Good—'cause he's going to be in your circus."

"How come? I mean, er—what does he do?"

"Nothing. He's just a freak—a sideshow freak. You can put him in a cage and call him 'The Ugliest Dog in the World.'" Rusty broke into a loud laugh. "I figure that's the sort of show a jerk like you can put on best—a freak show, get it? This'll probably be your star attraction!"

"Okay," Oliver said.

Rusty stopped laughing and put on his tough face.

"What do you mean 'okay'?" he growled. "I'm not asking if you like the idea. I'm just telling you that's how it's gonna be."

"Okay," Oliver said again, and added, "I mean, er—where'd you get him?"

"Found him," said Rusty. "He's just a stray. What'd you expect? Who'd want a dog that ugly?"

"I would!" said Andrew. He got down on his knees and started to hug and pet the dog.

"I'll bring Yuck around first thing in the morning," said Rusty. "You'd better have a cage all ready for him."

Whew! thought Oliver as Rusty walked down the drive, tugging Yuck behind him. Things were certainly moving along fast. So fast, they might get out of hand.

CHAPTER
5

When Saturday rolled around, Oliver bounced out of bed happily. He felt as eager and excited as when he'd first gotten the idea of putting on a circus.

It wasn't until he'd gulped down breakfast and hurried over to the Updegraffs' yard with Sam that he began to feel nervous about the show.

Mrs. Updegraff had said the circus performers could use her basement as a dressing room and backstage area. Soon the kids came trooping in.

Kim and Jennifer changed into their costumes. Then came Kim's brother Parnell with Squeeze Me, the boa constrictor. The musicians came in and changed into their school band uniforms. Then came Josh with his giraffe costume. Tim B. snuck in behind him.

"It's beginning to get crowded in here," Sam said.

"Give us some room, please," Josh said as he began to wiggle into the costume. "This isn't easy to get on."

He bent low to get into the neck part of the giraffe. The stiff neck swung around as Josh started to stand up, and the head thumped into a big bass drum.

"Oof!" said Josh. Kids ducked as the head swung the other way.

"Let's get out of here," Tim B. whispered from the other end of the costume. "They're laughing at us."

"Good idea," said Josh, heading carefully up the stairs. "Could somebody open the . . . ouch!" he exclaimed as the head crashed into the door.

"Don't worry," said Sam. "They'll be fine as long as they're out in the open."

But Oliver's heart was pounding as showtime drew closer. "Wh-wh-where's the t-tape deck?" he stammered.

"Josh set it up before he came down," Sam answered. "He even hooked it up to a bunch of amplifiers so the music will be louder."

"What about Bruiser?" asked Oliver.

"I've got him tied to a tree out back," said Wally. "Don't worry. Matthew and I will put on his mane in plenty of time for your lion-taming act. But there won't be any gorilla in the show."

Oliver frowned. "Why not?"

"Matthew's mom had it hanging outdoors to air out. Someone swiped it."

"Oh, great!" Oliver rolled his eyes.

"Calm down and stop fussing, Oliver," Sam scolded as she stuck on his fake mustache. She had borrowed her grandfather's silk hat for him to wear as ringmaster.

Oliver looked at himself in her mirror. "Hmm, not bad," he said, twirling his mustache.

Sam snapped her fingers. "We forgot to get Pierre and Jack Dempsey!"

"Hey, you're right!" Oliver's heart started thumping again. "I meant to go get 'em first thing this morning."

"Never mind, I'll ask if I can use the phone and call my dad. He can bring them over in our car."

Josh and Ambrose set up a refreshment stand under a tree. Nearly all the kids had been able to borrow wooden benches or lawn chairs or folding chairs from their parents. Parnell and Matthew were arranging these in half-circle rows. Kim and Jennifer, meanwhile, set up a table and chair for ticket-selling out in front.

By the time the audience started to arrive, Oliver had huge butterflies in his stomach. But at least the audience was a good size.

"Looks like we ought to make enough money to give the animal shelter a good start," Sam said. She was peeking out at the crowd from the basement door.

"Oops, wait!" She turned and glanced down the basement stairs at the performers. They had started to line up for the opening parade. "Where's Chad?"

Oliver grinned. "We lucked out—he's not going to be in the opening parade. Decided not to spring his act so soon. He says we should save the real show-stoppers for the climax."

Sam rolled her eyes.

Promptly at ten o'clock Oliver gave the signal to switch on the tape of march music. It was a piece called "Entrance of the Gladiators."

Linda led the way toward the center ring with her baton, followed by Dwayne Price tooting his trumpet and Jack Neely thumping a bass drum. They were both fifth-graders who belonged to the school orchestra.

Then came Oliver in his ringmaster's get-up, and the circus animals and the various performers. One by one they streamed out into view from the basement door. The animals got the biggest hand.

The audience cheered Pierre in his clown hat and ruff. He pranced along on his hind legs, a little American flag tied to one paw.

The Quigley twins, Bert and Bart, had rigged themselves up in a two-man horse costume. On top of their costume they carried a board, and Jennifer posed on it like a ballerina. She fluttered about in time to the music, then, "Eeeek!"

Jennifer slid off and landed on the grass. She ran after the horse.

Next came Kim, perched on a hollow papier-mâché elephant that Nick Angelotti and Al Rosen were holding up with both hands. The audience applauded.

Then everyone gasped. The giraffe had en-

tered. It marched along with great dignity. Oliver had to admit that Josh had come up with a terrific idea.

Suddenly the giraffe's neck started to wobble. Soon the whole animal began to zigzag.

"What's the matter?" Tim whispered from inside the giraffe. At least he *meant* to whisper. But with the band music blaring, he had to speak so loud that some of the audience could hear him too.

"Periscope came loose—can't see where I'm going!" Josh replied in a muffled voice.

Oliver groaned as the giraffe veered off the line of the parade. Its neck sagging sideways, the giraffe headed toward Mrs. Updegraff's garden pool.

"*Somebody stop them!*" Oliver hissed.

Too late! Before anyone could dash to the rescue, the giraffe toppled headfirst into the green water.

"Lay-deez and gentlemen! What a show we have for you today!" Oliver ad-libbed hastily. "What a show!"

The crowd roared. Darting a glance over his shoulder, Oliver saw the giraffe's rear end flee across the yard to hide behind the garage. The front end sat, dripping wet, on the ground.

"May I now present," Oliver shouted to get everyone's attention, "that world-famous acrobat—Ms. Samantha Lawrence—and her talented assistant, Ms. Jennifer Hayes!"

Wally pushed a portable gym into the center ring. Sam leaped up gracefully and grabbed the overhead horizontal bar. Then she began to swing and twirl at high speed while Jennifer did cartwheels on the ground.

From the bar Sam somersaulted to the ground, landing neatly on both feet. She took off in a series of back flips, and then walked up and down the side-porch steps on her hands.

The audience applauded. Oliver was proud of her. *Good old Sam!* he thought. *She looks just like an Olympic gymnast.*

Mrs. Updegraff was sitting in the front row like a queen on a throne, with Tweetums on her lap. She clapped in a refined way with the tips of her fingers. So did her husband, Ogden.

Matthew performed next. Oliver announced that here was one of the greatest juggling acts in the circus world. Matthew looked nervous. He started to juggle three oranges awkwardly.

Jack Neely nudged Oliver with his elbow and pointed upward. "Look!"

A gorilla had just appeared in the branches of one of the trees.

"Now we know what happened to that gorilla suit!" muttered Wally Perona.

Soon the audience noticed the hairy gate-crasher, too, and began to point and whisper. The gorilla was tossing rotten fruit down on Matthew.

"Who do you suppose it is?" Dwayne asked Oliver.

"Does the name Rusty Jackson ring a bell?" Oliver muttered between clenched teeth.

Matthew dropped one of his oranges when a rotten brown pear splashed in his face.

The other two oranges flew off. One hit the glass of lemonade on the arm of Mr. Updegraff's chair. It knocked the glass over, splashing lemonade on both him and Tweetums.

Mrs. Updegraff produced a handkerchief and dabbed the dog. She smiled a puckery little smile, as if to show that all was forgiven.

So did Mr. Updegraff.

The audience had fallen silent in embarrassment. Andrew began to giggle.

Matthew's cheeks flamed, and he bowed himself hastily out of the ring. Meanwhile, the gorilla swung off through the leafy tree tops.

Linda got things back on track with some expert baton-twirling. When she finished, Oriental music began booming out of the amplifiers, and Kim Williams came on to perform her snake-dance routine.

There were *oohs* and *aaahs* as Squeeze Me twined sinuously about her arms and body.

After winding up her act in a striking Cleopatra-like pose, Kim scampered off toward the garage to a loud round of applause.

Then Jack Dempsey and Princess Fluffy were brought out in a cat-sized boxing ring on top of an upturned garbage can.

Oliver dangled a key between them to start them pawing the air. But when he withdrew the key, the two cats began hissing and spitting at each other.

In no time Jack Dempsey chewed off one of

his boxing gloves and took a roundhouse swing at his opponent. Princess Fluffy sprang out of the boxing ring and streaked for the nearest bushes, pursued by anxious wails from Jennifer.

"Music! Quick!" Oliver signaled frantically. Dwayne blew some jazz riffs on his trumpet to distract the audience.

"And now for a thrilling, daredevil ride that will have you all on the edge of your seats!" cried Oliver with the toothiest smile he could manage.

Carmela Payton teetered around the ring twice on her unicycle before falling off. She got a sprinkling of polite applause.

Oliver was sweating as Sam hauled Bruiser forward on a leash. She unsnapped the leash and handed Oliver a whip, a hoop, and a carton of ice cream.

The lion-taming act started out fine, aside from the fact that Bruiser's mane was crooked. Bruiser sat up and begged. He reared up on his hind legs. He'd do anything for the ice cream Oliver fed him between cracks of the whip.

He even gave out a mournful howl that sounded like a sickly lion's roar when Oliver blew an ultrasonic dog whistle. Oliver cracked the whip harder.

Bruiser leaped up for the garbage can. He missed and knocked it over. Oliver hastily held up the hoop to coax Bruiser up on his feet again.

But Bruiser spotted Princess Fluffy coming out of the bushes. "Woof-woof-woof!" he bellowed as he charged across the yard. The chase was on!

Princess Fluffy dashed under the refreshment table. Bruiser smashed right through it. Popcorn and lemonade went flying in all directions.

"Won't *anything* go right?" Oliver groaned.

Wally whistled, and Bruiser ran over to him. They left the yard.

Oh, well, thought Oliver, trying to take a bright view, *at least the show was moving right along. Soon we'll be reaching our climax.*

But then the word *climax* made him think of Chad's Persian muscle dance. Oliver winced.

As he turned back to the ring to announce the next act, he spotted Jennifer. She was hurrying toward him with a nervous look on her face. Oliver felt a twinge of uneasiness.

"What's wrong?" he asked, not wanting to hear the answer.

"It's Kim," said Jennifer. "She can't find Squeeze Me! It must've gotten out of the garage!"

A scream pierced the air. Oliver's head swung around.

The boa was twining around Mrs. Updegraff's leg.

"Get this thing off me!" she shrieked at her husband.

Mr. Updegraff jumped up from his chair, twitching all over. He stared at his wife with a puzzled expression, as if not quite certain what to do next.

Mrs. Updegraff struggled to her feet, holding Tweetums high in the air. But the dog sprang

from her grasp. He landed safely and scuttled off under the bushes.

From there on things went so fast that Oliver could never quite remember exactly what happened.

At some point he became aware that the back door of the house was open. So he guessed that the Updegraffs' cook or one of the other servants must have popped out to see what all the commotion was about.

Kim and her brother were both struggling to pull Squeeze Me off Mrs. Updegraff's leg.

Suddenly, Squeeze Me uncoiled and went slithering off through the shrubbery.

Mrs. Updegraff, however, went right on shrieking.

"Tweetums! Where's Tweetums?" she screamed. "What's happened to poor little Tweetums?"

Kim yelled to her brother, "There's Squeeze Me! At the kitchen door. . . . Get him, Parnell!"

All eyes turned toward the Updegraffs' house. A snaky form was rearing up in the kitchen.

Oh no! gulped Oliver, his eyes widening. A bulge was working its way slowly down through the boa's body.

A shudder ran through the crowd. "*Oh, my goodness!*" a woman quavered in a shocked voice. "*Th-that poor little dog!*"

Mrs. Updegraff slumped to the ground in a faint.

CHAPTER
6

The people behind Mr. Updegraff helped him take care of his wife. Together, they managed to haul her back up on her chair. The Updegraffs' cook also came hurrying out with a damp cloth to place over Mrs. Updegraff's forehead.

Kim and Parnell rushed after Squeeze Me. By now the boa was creating panic inside the house.

"What're we going to do about—um—whatever it swallowed?" Kim asked.

"Are you kidding?" Parnell replied. "There's nothing we *can* do now!"

The cook was worming her way back into the kitchen through the crowd. She cried out.

"What's the matter?" Oliver asked her.

"That's no *dog*! That's my roast beef your stupid snake swallowed!"

The cook pointed her finger at an empty

roasting pan on the table. Oliver and Sam and Kim and Parnell sighed with relief.

"Will you kindly get that thing out of here!" the cook snapped at Kim and Parnell. They were struggling to keep hold of Squeeze Me.

"Yes, ma'am!" said Oliver. A path opened through the crowd like magic as they hustled the boa outside.

A hasty search began for Tweetums. "Here he is!" cried Sam. "Under the bushes!"

Oliver noticed Kathy Kellogg and a man with a hand-held video camera shooting everything in sight.

"Uh-oh!" Oliver nudged Josh and whispered. "Looks like Channel 12 just scored the news scoop of the year!"

Mrs. Updegraff was soon revived with smelling salts. She gathered Tweetums tearfully to her bosom. "Oh, my poor baby!" she cried in a choking voice. "You'll never know what your poor mama has just been through!"

Mr. Updegraff looked embarrassed.

Oliver gave a gloomy peek at Sam. "Well, there goes our circus," he murmured, "and maybe the Bartlett Woods Animal Shelter too!"

"Don't be silly," said Sam. "She hasn't seen her *nephew* perform yet. You think she's going to end the circus now?"

Oliver's face brightened. "Hey, you're right! Let's get going before she changes her mind!"

"Help me find Dwayne and Jack," he told Sam. "We'll need some noise to get everyone's attention!"

To add to the uproar, Oliver found Rusty Jackson teasing Andrew. Andrew had opened Yuck's cage so he could hug and pet him.

"Don't get too fond of him, kid," said Rusty. "Once this show's over, he's going to the dog pound—and you know what'll happen to him there! G-k-k-k!" He drew a finger across his throat.

"No, it *won't!*" Andrew yelled frantically. "He can stay in the animal shelter!"

"Are you kidding?" sneered Rusty. "Yuck'll be long gone before *that* ever gets built!"

Tears began to run down Andrew's cheeks as Rusty sauntered off, chuckling nastily.

"Hey, don't cry, Andrew," said Oliver. "There will too be an animal shelter! And besides, it still wouldn't be hard to find Yuck a new home— even if there wasn't a new shelter. Wanna know why?"

"*Why,* Oliver?!" Andrew exclaimed. His eyes grew big and hopeful, but his lower lip was still quivering.

Oliver could see that Andrew *wanted* to believe Yuck was in no danger—but he wasn't convinced by any means, and he might burst out sobbing again at any moment.

"Well, it's like this. I was looking in my—" Oliver broke off and stared Andrew right in the eye. "Wait a minute! First—can you keep a secret?"

Andrew nodded vigorously and crossed his heart.

"Well, okay, if that's a promise," said Oliver.

"As I started to tell you, the other day I was looking in my—"

Just then Josh came running up. "Dwayne and Jack are all set, Oliver! And Sam says to hurry up!"

"Okay, be right with you." Oliver turned to pat Andrew on the shoulder. "Stick around, Andrew, and I'll tell you what I found out soon as the show's over!"

Andrew's lower lip quivered harder than ever.

Dwayne and Jack trumpeted and thumped to get people's attention. The audience settled down again as Oliver cried, "On with the show!"

"And now, ladies and gentlemen," he announced, "keeping up our thrill-a-minute pace, we bring you the world's most sensational tightrope walk—featuring Ms. Samantha 'Twinkletoes' Lawrence!"

As far as Oliver was concerned, this was the real climax of the show. The tightrope was a garden hose stretched taut between two stepladders, with a pair of boys holding each stepladder in place.

As a hush fell over the audience, Sam climbed up one ladder. Then, using a bamboo pole for balancing, she walked, step by step, along the hose to the other ladder.

Her act brought thunderous applause.

Oliver felt silly reading the next introduction. It told how Chad Updegraff (who'd actually written the introduction himself) had spent "many moons in a Persian House of Strength." There he had developed a hero-type body, while learning the Dervishes' secrets of perfect muscular control.

Oliver could see Mrs. Updegraff perk up and beam at everyone. She looked as if she were taking personal credit for her nephew's amazing talent. She also twiddled her fingers gracefully in the air as the cameraman got ready to video tape it all for posterity.

A drum roll sounded over the amplifiers—then a pulse-pounding Oriental number that would have made good snake-charmer music for Kim.

Chad came bounding out of the basement door in what looked like pink and gold long underwear, and boots with curled-up toes. On his head was a feathered turban, and under his nose, a huge handlebar mustache.

But what caught everyone's eyes were his bulging *muscles*. At least that's what they were supposed to look like. Oliver knew that Chad was nowhere near the Mr. Universe class. The "muscles" had to be padding. Chad's skinny neck just didn't go with the rest of the image.

Between the fingers of each hand he was clutching three dumbbells. These looked impressive, except that Oliver had lifted them earlier and knew they were hollow.

He had to admit, though, that Chad could really twirl up a storm with those dummy weights. The way he pranced and leaped and spun around really had the audience's eyes popping.

Oliver felt a nudge. Dwayne hissed into his ear, "The gorilla's back!"

Oliver gave a startled look up at the tree.

What happened next was almost like a replay of what had happened to Matthew.

Something whizzed down from the tree top—only it wasn't a rotten pear, it was a ripe tomato. It hit Chad Updegraff in the mouth, splattering a gooey red mess all over his face and his gorgeous tights!

"*Awwwk!*" screamed Chad. His right foot went one way, his left foot the other—and his dumbbells went flying, just like Matthew's oranges. They sprayed through the air like shrapnel. One shot straight at the gorilla.

The gorilla tried to dodge it and stuck out an arm to ward off the dumbbell. He lost his balance and teetered wildly, then grabbed for another tree branch to steady himself.

Suddenly there was a loud cracking noise as the branch broke. The gorilla plopped to the ground with a thud. He picked himself up, groaning, and staggered off.

"Grab that gorilla!" cried Oliver.

Instantly Wally Perona tackled the gorilla as the crowd applauded.

It came as no surprise to Oliver that the gorilla was none other than Rusty Jackson. But Oliver himself had not the time to deal with such things now. *With or without the Whirling Dervish, the show must go on!* he thought.

"And now, to wind up this great circus spectacle," Oliver announced loudly, "we bring you

this *fantastic* animal specimen—a sight rarely seen by human eyes!"

Parnell had nailed together a strong wooden box-cage for Yuck. It had wire-fence netting all around, and roller-skate wheels underneath, so it could be rolled along. Sam had also borrowed a fancy-looking brown and silver tablecloth to drape over it to add an air of mystery.

Wally and Parnell wheeled the cage up to the center ring.

"Ladies and gentlemen," said Oliver. "I give you—*The Ugliest Dog in the World!*"

With a flourish he yanked off the cover. But as he looked at the audience, he noticed that their faces registered no surprise. If anything, the audience looked puzzled.

Oliver soon discovered why.

The cage was empty!

Yuck was gone!

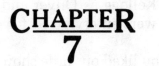

CHAPTER
7

It wasn't the greatest way to end a circus. But Oliver had no choice. As far as anyone could discover, Yuck was nowhere in Mrs. Updegraff's yard.

"Ladies and gentlemen, that concludes our show for this afternoon," said Oliver, looking a bit embarrassed. "We thank you all for coming and for helping us to start a fund to establish the Bartlett Woods Animal Shelter!"

Josh turned up the sound tape, and Dwayne and Jack joined in with trumpet and bass drum as the audience got up and started to leave.

At least none of them felt cheated, Oliver thought. He could tell that by their expressions. The show had been packed with riveting excitement from start to finish. In a way, even the mystery of what had happened to "The Ugliest

81

Dog in the World" added a special touch to the performance.

"Quite a spectacle you put on here today," said Kathy Kellogg as Oliver and Sam and the whole cast were interviewed for the television news.

"Happy you liked our little show," said Oliver.

It certainly hadn't been your ordinary, run-of-the-mill-type circus. But it was over at last, and Oliver could hardly wait for the yard to clear so he could solve the Mystery of the Missing Yuck.

By now Rusty had slunk off, after Matthew threatened to report him for swiping the gorilla suit.

"Think he could've turned Yuck loose, just to spoil the end of our show?" Sam puzzled.

Oliver shook his head. "Doesn't make sense—even for somebody as mean as Rusty. He was the one who made us put Yuck in our circus in the first place."

Oliver turned to Josh. "Any sign of Andrew?"

"Nope. We've looked all over the yard, even checked the house. He's not here."

Sam looked surprised and uneasy. "But I thought his mom told him to go home with you, Oliver."

"Exactly," said Oliver. "My guess is we've got a five-year-old runaway to track down—along with Yuck!"

"How come?" said Sam. Then her expression changed. "You mean *Andrew's* the one who let Yuck out of his cage?"

Oliver nodded. "Sure—and then took off with him. All because Rusty scared him into thinking Yuck was going to be taken to the pound and destroyed after the circus was over."

"That makes sense," agreed Josh. "But where would they go to hide?"

"Good question." Oliver clasped his hands behind his back and started pacing. "Andrew's a little dense in some ways. But he's probably smart enough to stay off the street. He knows that he and Yuck are easy to identify. They've probably gone to Arrowhead Park."

"Hey, right!" Sam exclaimed, punching her fist into her palm. "That's where he saw Yuck in the first place!"

"It's a pretty big park," Matthew observed gloomily.

"So let's get going!" said Josh.

Parnell had taken Squeeze Me home, but Kim and Jennifer and Wally offered to go along and help look.

The park was only a few blocks from Mrs. Updegraff's place. The search party spread out on both sides of the main park path, but there were a lot of woods to go through. By the time they got to the middle of the park, they all looked discouraged.

"Here, Andrew! Here, Yuck!" Jennifer shouted as she stood by the duck pond.

"What are you calling them for?" Sam asked. "They're not lost. They're running away. They're *hiding*, Jennifer."

"So?"

"So if you keep yelling, you'll only tip off Andrew that we're out searching for them."

"Oh." Jennifer was quiet for a second. "Then how are we ever going to find them?" she asked.

"That's the problem," said Sam, peering into some bushes. "It's going to start getting dark soon. Maybe we should call the police."

"Wait!" said Oliver. "I've got an idea!" He took out the ultrasonic whistle he'd used in his lion-taming act. "The sound it makes is too high-pitched for human ears to hear. But dogs can hear it. It made Bruiser howl. I don't know what effect it'll have on Yuck. But he may respond in some way or other that'll give away their hiding place—and Andrew won't even hear it."

As they fanned out and trudged up a hillside, Oliver kept blowing the whistle.

Nothing happened. They reached the top of the hill and looked all around. All they saw were trees. No dog, no little boy.

"Are you sure that thing is working?" Kim asked.

Oliver didn't answer. He just took a deep breath and blew another blast on the whistle.

"Listen!" said Sam. Just below them and to the right they heard a growl—then several barks.

Sam grinned hopefully. "Are we zeroing in?"

Oliver couldn't answer. He was still blowing on the whistle.

"I hope this doesn't turn out to be somebody else's dog," Jennifer said.

"Look!"

About halfway down the hill was a patch of blueberry bushes. Yuck was peering out at them from among the branches, and a small boy was lurking just behind him.

Mrs. Finch gave a joyful cry when she saw them coming back. She and Oliver's mother were waiting on the Moffitts' front porch. They had heard about the disappearing duo from some of the other children who had helped put on the circus. Mrs. Finch was just about to call the police when the search party turned up.

Oliver had been carrying Andrew piggyback for the last two blocks. Now he let him down, and Andrew ran up the porch steps and into his mother's arms.

"Oh, thank heavens you're all right!" she cried, hugging him tightly. She smiled at Oliver and his friends. "How can I ever thank you all for finding him!"

"No problem." Oliver beamed. "Just let Andrew keep the dog."

Mrs. Finch's smile slipped a bit at the sight of Yuck. But she came through in fine style. "Well, of course you can keep the dog, Andrew—even if he is a homely mutt!"

"Oh, no, this is no mutt, Mrs. Finch," said Oliver. "Actually he's a valuable purebred— probably worth quite a lot of money."

"Are you serious?" exclaimed Josh Burns.

"You bet I'm serious," said Oliver. "If you don't believe me, take a look in my animal encyclopedia. Yuck's a kind of dog you don't see often in America—at least not yet—but whenever one does appear in a dog show, it always makes a big hit. He's a Neapolitan mastiff."

Matthew stared at Yuck. "I guess dog-lovers will go for any kind if it's rare enough."

"They go for Neapolitan mastiffs," said Oliver. "That I guarantee."

Mrs. Finch looked startled. "In that case, Andrew," she said, "we'll keep Yuck provided his real owner doesn't turn up."

Yuck's tongue lolled out and he turned his massive head upward, staring soulfully at Andrew.

"Look at him!" said Sam. "I think he's actually *smiling* for a change!"

Over the weekend Josh had cranked out some LOST DOG signs on his word processor. Mr. and Mrs. Finch also paid for several newspaper ads.

When Monday rolled around, the kids heard that the town council was going to vote on setting up an animal shelter. All of Oliver's friends came over to sit on his porch and listen to the news channel on the radio. That's why they saw the yellow Rolls-Royce drive up in front of the Finches' house. Everyone gathered around as the chauffeur helped a young woman out of the car.

She looked like a fashion model or a movie actress. Sam nudged Oliver and said, "She sure didn't buy those clothes at the mall."

"Which of you is the one with the dog?" the woman inquired with a dazzling smile. Then as Andrew came out of the back yard with Yuck tagging along behind him, she beamed, "Ah, yes! Here they come now, I see."

To no one in particular she added brightly, "I'm Yolande Yates. Maybe some of you or your mothers have seen me on television in the afternoon."

"Mom never watches soap operas," said Sam. "Neither do I."

Ms. Yates's smile tightened. She turned away from Sam and spoke to Andrew. "Well, anyhow, dear, I've been away on vacation, down in Acapulco. That's in Mexico, you see, quite far from here. So, of course, I had to leave Rodolfo in a kennel near my country home. But he's such a big strong brute, he broke loose the very next day!"

She patted Yuck on the head.

"Of course, I had no idea he'd gotten out. Mr. Devoe, the kennel owner, was simply frantic! He was afraid I might sue him, I suppose, so he's been searching all over and offering an immense reward for information leading to Rodolfo's return. But it never occurred to him that the dog would have strayed this far. When I got back from Mexico, I bought *all* the papers and saw your parents' ad—so here I am!"

Andrew looked down at the ground. With a sigh Yolande Yates gave up trying to talk to him. She signaled her chauffeur, and he prodded Yuck into the Rolls. With a parting kiss on the cheek, she tried to press some money into Andrew's hand.

"So, dear! Do say hello to your mummy and daddy—and thank you all for taking such splendid care of Rodolfo. I feel it was especially kindhearted of you, considering that he's such an ugly-looking old thing!"

Andrew began to sob. Just then, Yuck ran out of the car. Andrew threw his arms around Yuck as Yolande stared in surprise.

"My dear child! What's all this? Do you actually mean you'd like to keep this hulking beast?"

"Yes, yes! Please don't take him away!"

"Well, of course not, dear, if that will make you happy! . . . May I tell you a tiny secret?"

Yolande flashed another dazzling smile. "To be quite frank, I've never really cared for Rodolfo. But, you see, he was a present from a friend, so it was rather embarrassing to admit that the dog's looks almost made me ill. Now I can explain that you loved him so much that I just *couldn't* bring myself to break your heart by taking him away from you. Keep the ugly old thing for your very own doggie—plus the reward from me—and I shall also see that you collect the reward posted by the Devoe Kennels!"

"Hey, now, wait a minute!"

Oliver winced as he heard Rusty Jackson's voice. Rusty was crowding behind him, pushing his way forward to squawk at Yolande Yates.

"Maybe you don't know it, lady, but *I'm* the one who found your dog—so I'm the one who

should get the reward! And what's more, I want to keep him myself!"

"Yeah, sure," Sam cut in. A chorus of jeers at Rusty came from the other children.

"You're the one who would've sent him to the pound if Andrew hadn't saved him," Sam went on. "You even named him Yuck—that's how much you care for him."

"Be quiet, big mouth!" said Rusty. "Today I spotted that ad in the paper from the Devoe Kennels and called them! The man said you were coming here to the Finches', so I rushed over right away."

He held out one hand and blabbered on. "I'll take the reward money right now, Miss Yates— okay? And then I'll take the dog home."

Yolande Yates frowned and tapped her cheek with one finger for a moment. "Hang on to the dog," she told her chauffeur. She smiled sweetly at both Rusty and Andrew.

"Well, children," she said, "I think there's only one way to settle this, and that is to let Rodolfo choose whom he wants to belong to."

"What do you mean?" Rusty demanded.

"You can each call him, and we'll see which one he goes to. Okay?"

A sly smile spread over Rusty's face. "Great idea! That'll suit me fine!"

Oliver watched as Rusty pulled a copy of the Devoe Kennels' newspaper ad about the lost Neapolitan mastiff out of his pocket. He turned his back and showed it to his pal, Jay Goodman.

The ad said: Answers to the name Rudy!

Oliver and Sam peeked at it over Rusty's shoulder. Sam opened her mouth, but Oliver put a finger to his lips.

"Very well—go ahead, please," said Yolande Yates. She signaled her chauffeur to let go of the mastiff's collar.

"Here, Rudy, Rudy!" Rusty called out. He grinned confidently. "Come on, Rudy boy!"

Oliver and his friends held their breath. Rusty looked as if he knew exactly what he was doing. Was Andrew about to lose his pet?

Yuck looked at Rusty but didn't move.

Rusty lost some of his grin. "Come on, Yuck!" he blurted out, still trying to sound sure of himself. "Here, Yuck boy! Come here, Yuck!"

Yuck stayed right where he was.

Andrew held out his arms. "Here, Bluey! Here, boy!"

Yuck sprang up and trotted straight into Andrew's arms. His big tongue happily licked Andrew's face.

Oliver and Sam were astonished to see a tear trickle down Yolande Yates's face. "Well! I guess that settles it," she murmured, dabbing her eyes and nose with a lace handkerchief.

She beamed a final dazzling smile at everyone, handed the reward to Andrew, and climbed into her Rolls.

Rusty stared open-mouthed as the big car pulled away. Then he turned to Andrew. "You little creep," he said. "You robbed me! That reward should be mine!" He stepped forward, making a fist.

Yuck looked up and growled, showing his teeth.

Rusty froze.

"I wouldn't go around yelling about robberies," said Oliver. "Or someone might start asking how that gorilla suit disappeared from the Farleys' house and wound up on you."

"I . . . it . . ." Rusty didn't know what to say. Oliver had him cold.

Just then, the Channel 12 news van came rolling down the street. The door opened, and Kathy Kellogg sprang out. "Oliver! Sam!" she called. "Have you heard?"

"What?" said Oliver.

"The town council has voted unanimously to establish the Bartlett Woods Animal Shelter for strays," she said. "They're using the vacant lot near the park. It will be fenced in, cleaned up, and the garage building will be repainted and repaired."

"That's great!" said Sam.

"Well, there are a few people here who'd like to thank you." Climbing out of the van was Mrs. Rosebury, followed by several of her pets. The cameraman was taking in the whole scene.

Mrs. Rosebury was smiling with joy as she hugged Sam and Oliver. Pierre pranced about happily on his hind legs. "Thank you so much, children," Mrs. Rosebury said. "At last my little friends will have a home!"

Everyone cheered, Kathy Kellogg said a few words, and then the van took off to bring Mrs. Rosebury and her animal friends home.

Rusty Jackson broke away from the crowd, muttering, "You guys get on TV, and I get nothing. You always cheat me out of anything good!"

"Wait a second," called Oliver. "That's not true. We've got a job to do today at a rich person's house, and we're really going to clean up. Want to come along?"

"Sure!" said Rusty. "Where are we going?"

"To the Updegraffs," Oliver answered. "There's still a lot of trash around, and I'm sure you'll pick up more than your fair share."

Even Yuck had to laugh at that.